MW00947876

THE

PUMPKIN PAINTER

THE
PUMPKIN PAINTER

Jennifer Matthai Garner

illustrated by Stephanie Mullani

Tru Publishing
2939 S Mayflower Way
Boise, ID 83709

Library of Congress Control Number: 2015952206
ISBN (paperback): 978-1-941420-13-3
ISBN (hardcover): 978-1-941420-14-0

1 2 3 4 5 6 19 18 17 16 15
1st edition, October 2015

Printed in the United States of America

Cover and Interior Design — Tru Publishing
www.trupublishing.com

Editing — Kim Foster
www.kimfostereditor.com

Dedication

I would like to dedicate this book to the memory of my mother, Virginia May Dean, whose heart was filled with kindness and song.

Far away, in a magical forest, there once lived a grandmother and a grandfather. They looked like ordinary grandparents, but they were not ordinary at all. For you see, Mama Louisa and Papa Louis had the recipes for happiness etched upon their hearts.

One day they discovered that they could share their happiness with their friends, for they had a garden of goodness sitting right on their pantry shelves. They would simply stir a little love, a dash of joy, a pinch of peace, and a sprinkle of kindness into each day, and goodness would begin to grow.

Mama Louisa and Papa Louis often invited their young friends to gather around their kitchen table where they would stir up the recipes for happiness.

love peace Kindness

joy

And this is where
The story begins

Papa Louis spent his days harvesting his precious pumpkin patch. The pumpkin patch was filled with all sorts of pumpkins, and Papa Louis was thankful for such a great variety. He loved all of the pumpkins: big pumpkins, little pumpkins, round pumpkins, tall pumpkins, and even the odd pumpkins. In fact, when Papa Louis harvested the pumpkin crop, it made him appreciate all the different friends in the forest family.

Just as each pumpkin was precious and unique, every creature in the Magic Forest was precious and unique. And so every day, as Papa Louis harvested the pumpkins, he was filled with thankfulness for such a colorful variety of forest friends. He even made up a little pumpkin song which he sang as he worked in his precious pumpkin patch:

Papa loves the little pumpkins,
All the pumpkins in his patch,
Big and little, round and tall,
Papa knows and loves them all.
Papa loves the many pumpkins in his patch.

Mama Louisa was also doing a bit of her own harvesting. As the forest families had gathered together, time and time again, in her little cabin to stir up stories, she had been busy tending the goodness that was beginning to grow in their hearts. The families still had so much to learn, but Mama Louisa rejoiced every time she saw an act of kindness. She even made up a little song which she sang as she knit their winter hats and gloves:

Loving deeds are filled with magic,
Growing hearts need lots of love,
When you see a lonely creature,
Shower him with many hugs.

The youngest members of the forest family were very, very busy collecting nuts for their winter storehouse. They were having such fun working together as good friends often do.

Hopson, Bopson and Dopson, the bird children, would fly into the branches of the tall oak trees and knock the nuts off the branches down to their waiting friends. Esma, Nesma and Besma, the squirrel children, would scurry about to gather the fallen nuts and sort them into piles of ten. This was busy, busy work. It seemed there were more nuts than ever before.

One afternoon, when the young forest friends were playing and working together, a nut accidently landed on the top of a beautiful gourd and out popped a very small, very strange, and extremely odd, little man. They had never

seen this odd little man, and he was no ordinary forest creature. He was dressed in strange striped clothing and wore a funny pointed hat.

He stood with his little hands on his little hips and he yelled, "Prickly little pips! Go away or I'll eat you and your nuts!" He wasn't being nice at all and the forest friends decided in an instant that they didn't like him. They began to wonder,

W hy was he here?

Where did he come from?

Now sometimes even nice little forest children can say unkind words. Hopson, Dopson and Bopson began to sing, "Go away mean little man. You don't belong here." The squirrel children who also loved to sing quickly joined this crooked chorus.

Mama Louisa and Papa Louis heard the commotion of the crooked chorus echoing throughout the forest. They came at once to help their young forest friends resolve their differences.

"These are not the words of friends, dear children," said Papa Louis.

"He doesn't belong here," answered Hopson.

"If he is standing in the Magic Forest then he belongs here," replied Papa Louis, "for every creature is here for a reason. Perhaps he has been sent to teach us a lesson."

It was a day in late autumn when this quarrel occurred.

Mama Louisa and Papa Louis had been harvesting pumpkins that day,

But as they listened to this squabble they put the pumpkins away.

They knew just what to do and just what to say.

ama Louisa stirred up these muffins ...

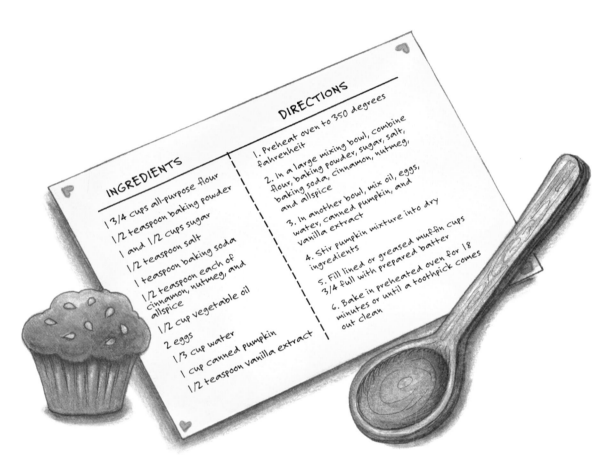

INGREDIENTS

1 3/4 cups all-purpose flour
1/2 teaspoon baking powder
1 and 1/2 cups sugar
1/2 teaspoon salt
1 teaspoon baking soda
1/2 teaspoon each of cinnamon, nutmeg, and allspice
1/2 cup vegetable oil
2 eggs
1/3 cup water
1 cup canned pumpkin
1/2 teaspoon vanilla extract

DIRECTIONS

1. Preheat oven to 350 degrees fahrenheit

2. In a large mixing bowl, combine flour, baking powder, sugar, salt, baking soda, cinnamon, nutmeg, and allspice

3. In another bowl, mix oil, eggs, water, canned pumpkin, and vanilla extract

4. Stir pumpkin mixture into dry ingredients

5. Fill lined or greased muffin cups 3/4 full with prepared batter

6. Bake in preheated oven for 18 minutes or until a toothpick comes out clean

 *Sing a song of goodness,*
Add a bit of care,
Mix it all together,
With others we will share.

Once we get to baking,
Together we are one,
Loving, thanking, food we're making,
Time with ones we love.

nd Papa Louis told a story, that I'll share with you today.

Once upon a time, in a rich fertile land, there grew a gigantic pumpkin. So big was this vegetable that it could take a man half a day to walk around the pumpkin's perimeter. It was estimated to be eighteen deckles high and twenty-four deckles around.

Now word spread about this enormous pumpkin and people came from near and far just to marvel at its size. The pumpkin sat right in the middle of a very deep valley, surrounded on all sides by mountains. In order to visit the Gargantuan Pumpkin, you had to climb up the snow-capped mountains and then travel down the steep slopes into the Great Valley of the Pumpkin. It was a long and difficult journey.

But the pumpkin peekers came anyway. Some came for the thrill and others came out of curiosity. It was, in fact, a remarkable vegetable. Not only was it enormous, but it was also multi-colored. Some of the pumpkin peekers would stand in the Great Valley and marvel at the pumpkin's perfect beauty, because they knew it was a magical pumpkin. But others would shake their heads in disgust and call it a worthless creation, because it wasn't an ordinary orange pumpkin. There were always the same questions:

Why is it here?

Where did it come from?

The sun shone brightly for forty days. This long stretch of golden days marked the end of the long warm season and the beginning of the cool autumn season. And all the while, the pumpkin peekers gathered in the Great Valley to see the Gargantuan Pumpkin.

Some came to measure the pumpkin with their fancy measuring sticks. Others came to collect soil samples to calculate the ground's rich nutrients. The positive pumpkin peekers glowed with goodness as they marveled at the beauty of this unusual vegetable. But the peevish pumpkin peekers didn't like the pumpkin because it was different.

The sun smiled down on their attempts to understand this remarkable, yet unfathomable, act of Mother Nature.

On the eve of the fortieth day, while the pumpkin peekers sat around their campfires discussing their newest Gargantuan Pumpkin theories, the earth began to rumble. Father Winter was beginning to wake from his long summer sleep. As he stretched this way and that, he yawned a big, deep, white yawn, sending a freezing cold breeze through the Great Valley.

Father Winter's yawn blew a great number of rain clouds over the mountains into the Great Valley. Darkness filled the valley and the rain clouds began to cry. It was a long cold rain that fell on the eve of the fortieth day. As Father Winter continued to stretch this way and that, the ground shook and rumbled until a crack appeared around the top of the huge pumpkin's shell.

The trees clapped their leaves, the wind whistled, and the moonlight lit up the Great Valley of the Gargantuan Pumpkin.

The pumpkin peekers were in for a colorful treat.

They didn't know that Peter Peter Pumpkin Painter was just flying over the snow-capped mountains. He was dressed all in orange, from his head to his toes, and he carried a paintbrush full of colorful rainbows.

For a moment, time stood still, as Peter Peter Pumpkin Painter removed the cap of his great paint jar. He took his giant paintbrush and stirred the colors of fall into the Gargantuan Pumpkin. Then he began to paint the tree-lined valley.

He took his mighty paintbrush, dipped it into the Gargantuan Pumpkin and drew out the first color of fall – red.

As Peter Peter Pumpkin Painter brushed the bright red paint across the treetops, the positive pumpkin peekers gasped in awe, for the trees were draped with dignity.

With the next dip, he drew out the second color of fall – yellow. As he spread the bright yellow paint across the trees of the Great Valley, even the peevish pumpkin peekers smiled with delight, for the trees began to shine just like the rising sun.

With a third dip, Peter Peter Pumpkin Painter drew out the last fall color – orange. As he swept the bright orange across the treetops, the pumpkin peekers sang a song of fall colors.

Peter Peter Pumpkin Painter,
Father Winter's entertainer,
Paints the forest orange and brown,
Autumn colors all rain down.
With a colorful touch and his magic paintbrush
The forest becomes autumn in a rush.

The forest had been magically transformed into an autumn rainbow!

Peter Peter Pumpkin Painter bid them farewell, for he was off to paint the world with his fall colors.

The trees clapped their leaves, the wind whistled and the sunrise lit up the magical autumn landscape.

When Papa Louis finished telling the story, Mama Louisa came out of the cottage carrying a basket filled with a fresh batch of Positively Perfect Pumpkin Muffins.

"Dear children", Mama Louisa kindly concluded, "The Magic Forest is filled with all sorts of creatures and we need to be thankful for such a colorful variety. Every creature in the Magic Forest is precious and special. Let us be thankful that we are all different. Our new friend deserves a friendly forest welcome and a warm pumpkin muffin."

A scent of goodness filled the cottage that day,
and no little squabble could take it away,
Friendship filled up every inch in that room,
as the forest friends sang the Pumpkin Painter tune:

Peter Peter Pumpkin Painter,
Father Winter's entertainer,
Paints the forest orange and brown
Autumn colors all rain down.
With a colorful touch and his magic paintbrush
The forest becomes autumn in a rush.

Remember ...

It Takes Many Colors to Make Our World Magical!

RECIPE

Positively Perfect Pumpkin Muffins

Ingredients:

1 and 3/4 cups all-purpose flour

1/2 teaspoon baking powder

1 and 1/2 cups sugar

1/2 teaspoon salt

1 teaspoon baking soda

1/2 teaspoon each of cinnamon, nutmeg, and allspice

1/2 cup vegetable oil

2 eggs

1/3 cup water

1 cup canned pumpkin

1/2 teaspoon vanilla extract

Mama Louisa sometimes stirs in a 1/2 cup of pecans, currants, raisins, or walnuts

Directions:

1. Preheat oven to 350 degrees fahrenheit.

2. In a large mixing bowl, combine flour, baking powder, sugar, salt, baking soda, cinnamon, nutmeg, and allspice.

3. In another bowl, mix oil, eggs, water, canned pumpkin, and vanilla extract.

4. Stir pumpkin mixture into dry ingredients.

5. Fill lined or greased muffin cups 3/4 full with prepared batter.

6. Bake in preheated oven for 18 minutes or until a toothpick comes out clean.

SONGS

PAPA LOVES THE LITTLE PUMPKINS

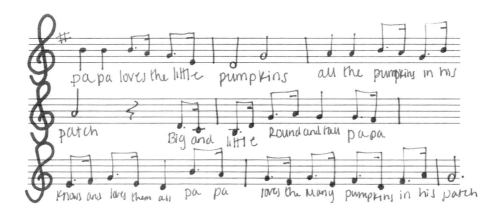

LOVING HEARTS

SONG OF GOODNESS

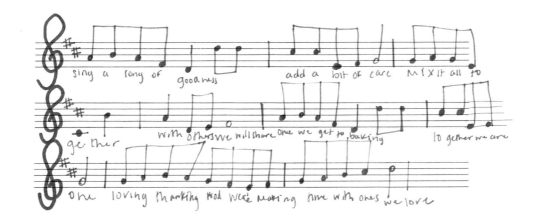

PUMPKIN PAINTER

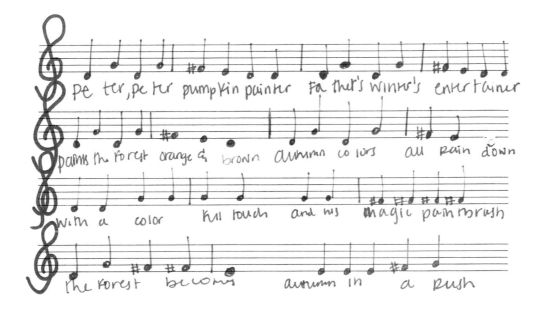

Acknowledgements

I would like to thank:

My husband, Bruce, for his support and encouragment.

Emily, for helping with the songs and putting them to music.

Molly-Kate, for drawing preliminary sketches and helping with the editing process.

Elizabeth, for baking several batches of pumpkin muffins to find the perfect batch.

Alex, for his unparalleled optimism.

Stella and Cecilia, for their taste-testing and story listening.

Stephanie, for bringing my characters to life.

And Kim, for editing the first Mama Louisa and Papa Louis story.

About the Author

 **Jennifer Matthai Garner** has been stirring up goodness with her own six children for the past 25 years. She was inspired to create the Mama Louisa and Papa Louis stories while baking bread with her children and their preschool friends. She is a passionate children's writer who draws inspiration from the mountains of North Carolina and aspires to publish the entire series of Mama Louisa and Papa Louis Cozy Cottage Stories.

She currently homeschools her two youngest children while living in western Idaho with her husband, Bruce, two dogs, one cat and five chickens.